A NOTE TO PARENTS

When your children are ready to "step into reading," giving them the right books is as crucial as giving them the right food to eat. **Step into Reading Books** present exciting stories and information reinforced with lively, colorful illustrations that make learning to read fun, satisfying, and worthwhile. They are priced so that acquiring an entire library of them is affordable. And they are beginning readers with a difference—they're written on five levels.

Early Step into Reading Books are designed for brand-new readers, with large type and only one or two lines of very simple text per page. **Step 1 Books** feature the same easy-to-read type as the Early Step into Reading Books, but with more words per page. **Step 2 Books** are both longer and slightly more difficult, while **Step 3 Books** introduce readers to paragraphs and fully developed plot lines. **Step 4 Books** offer exciting nonfiction for the increasingly independent reader.

The grade levels assigned to the five steps—preschool through kindergarten for the Early Books, preschool through grade 1 for Step 1, grades 1 through 3 for Step 2, grades 2 through 3 for Step 3, and grades 2 through 4 for Step 4—are intended only as guides. Some children move through all five steps very rapidly; others climb the steps over a period of several years. Either way, these books will help your child "step into reading" in style!

Copyright © 2001 Universal Studios Publishing Rights, a division of
Universal Studios Licensing, Inc. The movie *Dr. Seuss' How the Grinch Stole
Christmas!* © 2000 Universal Studios. Based on the book *How the Grinch Stole
Christmas!* book and characters ™ & © Dr. Seuss Enterprises, L.P. 1957, renewed
1985. All rights reserved under International and Pan-American Copyright
Conventions. Published in the United States by Random House, Inc., New York,
and simultaneously in Canada by Random House of Canada Limited, Toronto.

www.randomhouse.com/seussville   www.universalstudios.com

Library of Congress Cataloging-in-Publication Data:
Worth, Bonnie. How the Grinch got so grinchy / by Bonnie Worth ; illustrated
by Ray Goudey.
   p.   cm. — (Step into reading, a step 2 book)
"Based on How the Grinch stole Christmas! by Dr. Seuss."
SUMMARY: The story of how unkind treatment and an unhappy Christmas turned
the Grinch into a mean-spirited fellow who plagued the Whos.
ISBN 0-375-80662-8 (trade) — ISBN 0-375-90662-2 (lib. bdg.)
[1. Behavior—Fiction. 2. Christmas—Fiction. 3. Stories in rhyme.]
I. Goudey, Ray, ill. II. Seuss, Dr. How the Grinch stole Christmas! III. Title.
IV. Step into reading. Step 2 book. PZ8.3.W896 Ho 2001 [E]—dc21 00-037296

Printed in the United States of America September 2001 10 9 8 7 6 5 4 3 2 1

RANDOM HOUSE, the Random House colophon, and STEP INTO READING are
registered trademarks and the Step into Reading colophon is a trademark of
Random House, Inc.

Step into Reading®

How the Grinch Got So Grinchy

By Bonnie Worth

Illustrated by Ray Goudey

Based on the motion picture screenplay
by Jeffrey Price & Peter S. Seaman

Based on the book by Dr. Seuss

A Step 2 Book

Random House 🏠 New York

Unlike the Whos,

who liked Christmas a lot,

the Grinch in his cave

on Mt. Crumpit DID NOT!

"He was born to hate Christmas,"

most people will say.

But maybe his life was

what made him that way.

'Twas the night before Christmas,

quite some time ago.

The night new Who babies

fell down with the snow.

They fell down to earth

on their soft pumbrasellas,

these little Who gals

and these little Who fellas.

The Who parents greeted

each bundle of joy,

except for this one

somewhat sad little boy.

No Who seemed to hear him,

or want him, or need him.

No Who came to hug him,

or clean him, or feed him.

At long last, two Who gals

came out and they found

the source of a most

un-adorable sound.

They got down the baby,

who hung in a tree.

They pulled back the blanket...

and what did they see?

A fuzz-covered baby!

Yes, fuzzed! Every inch!

He wasn't a Who,

so they called him a Grinch!

The two gals, they fed him,

and cleaned him, and oiled him.

They fussed over him—

yes, those gals really spoiled him.

The Grinch was their pride
and the Grinch was their joy.
They treated him like
any other Who boy.

With all of his fuzz,

he was really quite cute!

Come winter, he went out…

...without a snowsuit!
Yes, life for the boy
was dandy and cool...

...until the first day of
his life at Who school.

The students, they stared,

and they teased him as well.

They made fun of his fangs

and his funky Grinch smell.

The teacher, Miss Rue Who,

whose job was to teach him,

was not very good,

but she still tried to reach him.

She drummed in the lesson

that every Who knows,

from the ends of their hairs

to the tips of their toes:

Put Christmas ahead

of all other Who days.

Make Christmas your mission

in millions of ways.

Deck every hall

and shop till you drop.

Jingle those bells

and don't you DARE stop!

"Is it all really worth it?"
the Grinch had to mutter.
And then something happened
to make his heart flutter.

Young Martha May Whovier
was staring and winking.
"Could she really like me?"
the Grinch started thinking.

"Whobilation's tomorrow,"
Miss Rue Who told the gang
as she slammed the book shut
and the Who school bell rang.

"Bring in a present

for a special someWho.

Go out and shop!

Show what you can do!"

He went home and worked
with some junk that he had.
For a bunch of old junk,
it did not look so bad!

"This angel will sit
on the top of her tree.
Whenever she sees it,
she will think of me."

He found an old razor
inside an old sack.

He started to scrape
and he started to hack.

36

So bad was the job

that he did on his face,

the next day he hid

from the whole Whoman race.

Miss Rue Who took one look

at the Grinch and she said:

"Please take that paper bag

off of your head."

Now, August May Who

(who would one day be mayor)

liked Martha May, too,

and he did not play fair.

"This guy must be under
some kind of a curse.
The face or the gift—
I can't tell which is worse!"

The Who gang went bonkers.

They laughed and they jeered.

"May Who's a boss Who!"

was the cheer they all cheered.

"Your Christmas is stupid!"
the Grinch then cried out.
He started to scream
and he started to shout.
He started to jump
and he started to thrash,
until all that he touched
had been turned into trash.

So off the Grinch went
to a cave on Mt. Crumpit.
And as for the Whos,
they could like it or lump it!
He stayed in his cave
with a sneer on his face,
hating the Whos
and the whole Whoman race.

He lived all alone—

yes, these are the facts—

except for his cute

little puppy dog, Max.

So whenever the meaning
of Christmas gets hazy
and the seasonal crunch
makes you go a bit crazy,
just think of the Grinch
in his cave far away
and remember that he
wasn't always that way.

And forget all the things
you have read or have heard.
The Grinch needs a friend
and he NEEDS a kind word.